For Cher

Text and illustrations © 2004 by Mo Willems

This book is hand-lettered by Mo Willems, with additional text set in Helvetica Neue LT Pro and Latino Rumba/Monotype.

Special Edition, April 2013

10 9 8 7

FAC-039745-21036

Printed in South Korea

Library of Congress Control Number for Hardcover Edition: 2003050908

ISBN 978-1-4231-8372-3

Visit www.hyperionbooksforchildren.com and www.pigeonpresents.com

The Pigeon Finds a Hot Dog!

words and pictures by mo willems

HYPERION BOOKS FOR CHILDREN / New York

I've never
had a
hot dog
before....

What do they taste like?

Each morsel is a joy! A celebration in a bun!

Of course! Enjoy!

Go
ahead.

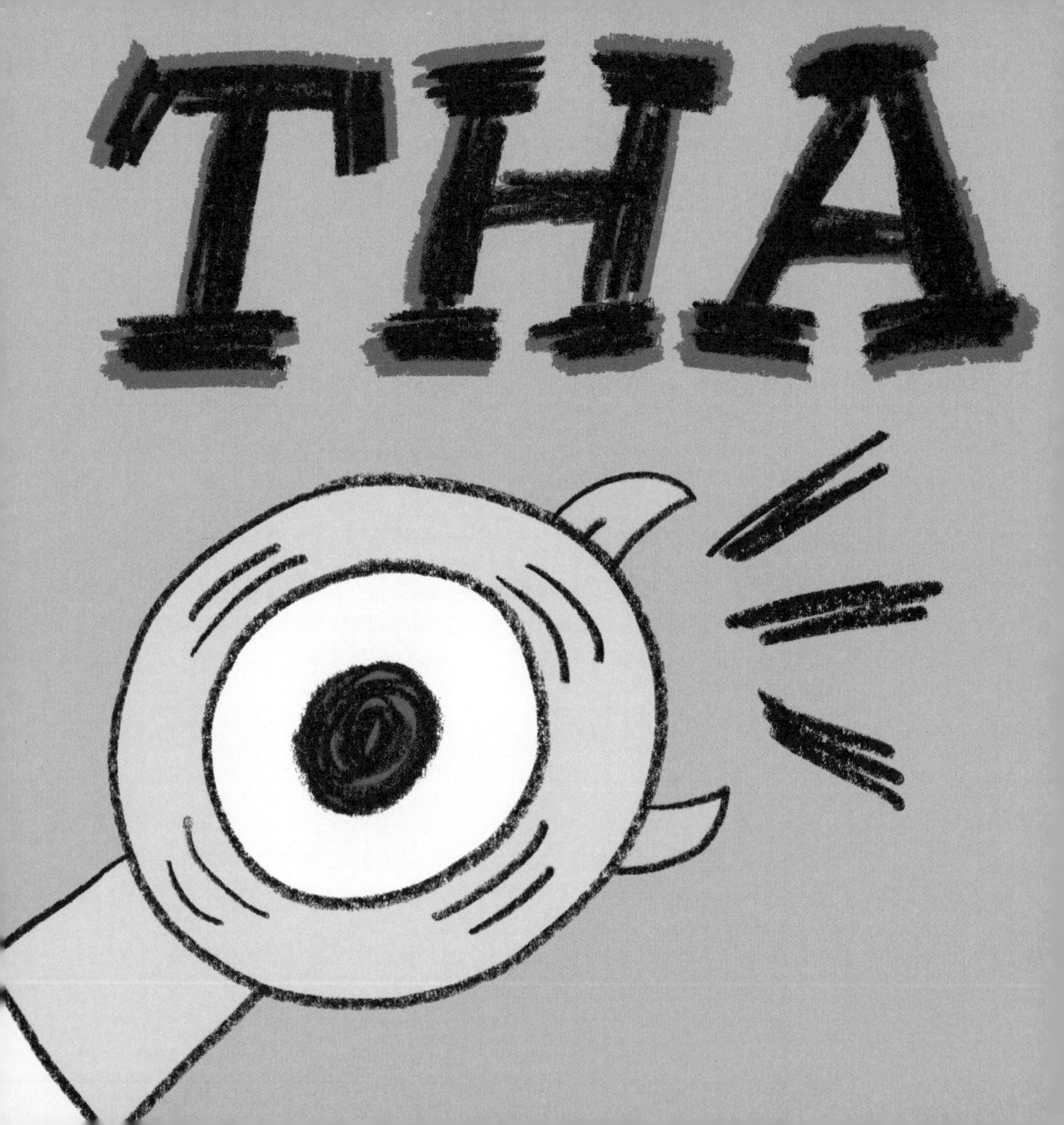
THA

T'S
IT!

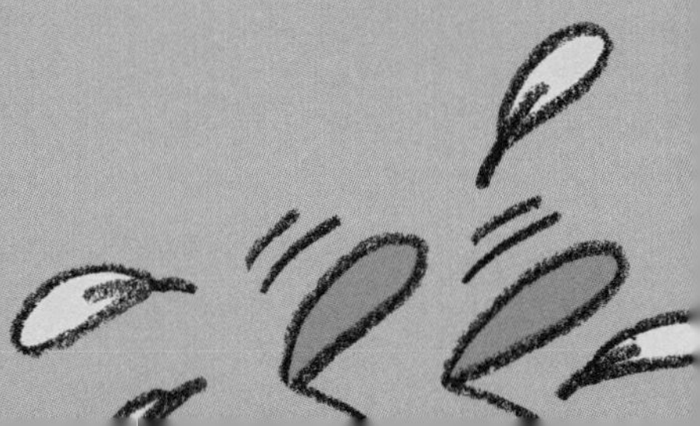

I think
I've got
an idea.

You know, you're pretty smart for a duckling.

Hmmm...
needs
mustard.

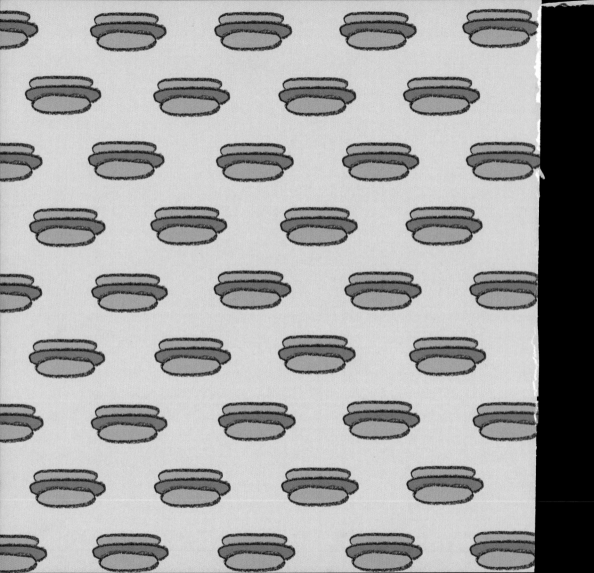